Pocahontas

Ariel

The Princess Encyclopedia

Mulan

Belle

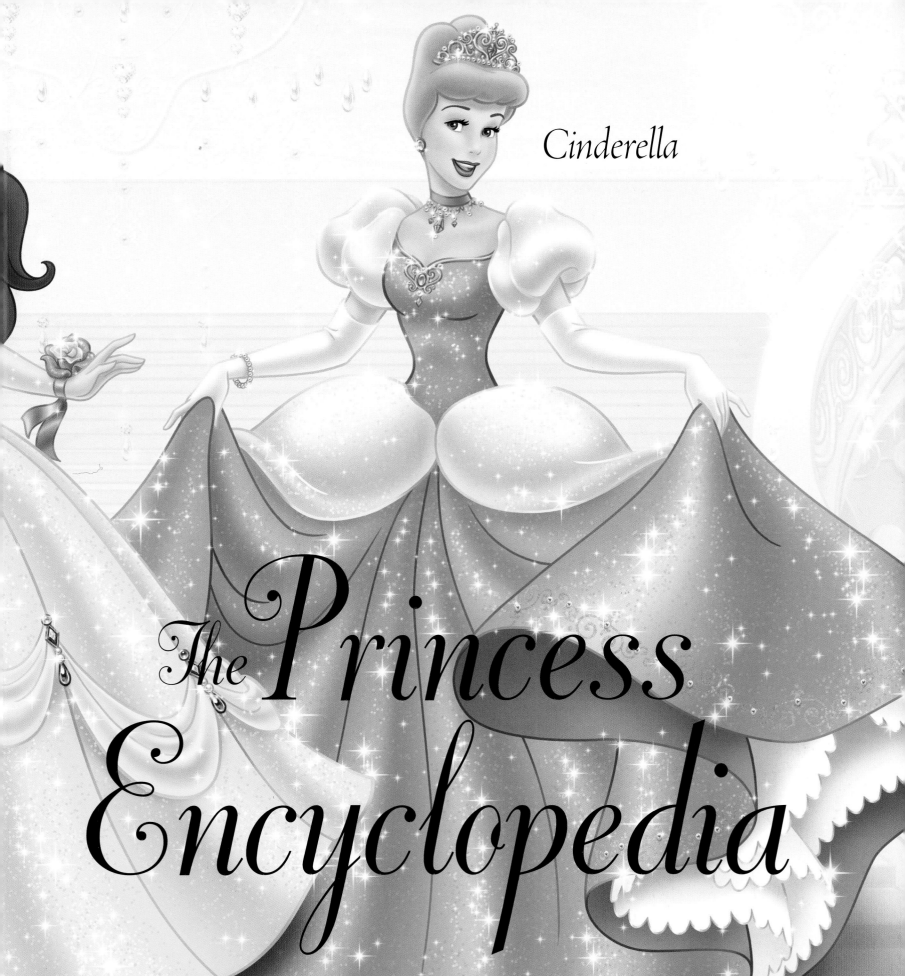

Cinderella

The Princess Encyclopedia

Written by Jo Casey, Beth Landis Hester, and Catherine Saunders

Contents

Aurora

Tiana

Jasmine

Ride into battle with brave **Mulan**. She will do everything to make her family proud…

Take a look at kind **Cinderella.** Life is tough for her until a fairy godmother waves her magic wand…

Meet the Princesses

Welcome to the world of princesses! You'll discover a wonderful place full of romance, adventure, beauty, and, of course, just a little magic.

Spend some time with caring **Aurora**. She is always dreaming of True Love's Kiss…

Take a leaf out of beautiful **Belle's** book. She is brave enough to find true love in the unlikeliest place…

Share a magical adventure with determined **Jasmine**. She won't marry a prince she doesn't love…

Journey under the sea and meet curious Ariel. She can't wait to find out what it is like to be human…

Dare to follow independent Pocahontas. She just knows that something exciting is about to happen to her…

You'll find out everything you ever wanted to know about your favorite princesses, from beautiful gowns to fantastic friends and from handsome princes to happy endings. Let the magical journey begin!

Get to know gentle Snow White. Her wicked stepmother will do anything to make sure Snow White is not the fairest in the land…

Learn a valuable lesson with Tiana. Sometimes kissing a frog isn't such a bad idea after all…

Snow White's Story

Once Upon a Time...

...there lived a kind princess named Snow White. Snow White lived in a castle with her cruel stepmother, the Queen, who forced her to work as her servant. But the gentle princess believed that one day a prince would rescue her and they would live happily ever after together.

One day, Snow White made a wish at the wishing well for a prince to find her and suddenly a prince appeared! He had heard the sound of Snow White's singing and when he saw the maiden he fell in love.

The wicked Queen was jealous of Snow White's grace and beauty. When her Magic Mirror told her that Snow White was the fairest in the land, the Queen ordered her Huntsman to kill the girl. He couldn't hurt Snow White and instead begged her to run away. Frightened, Snow White ran into the dark forest and collapsed in tears.

When she woke up, she was surrounded by friendly animals. They took her to the Seven Dwarfs' cottage where she would be safe. Doc, Grumpy, Sneezy, Happy, Dopey, Sleepy, and Bashful were surprised to find Snow White in their home, but happy that she had cooked and cleaned for them!

The Seven Dwarfs quickly grew to love the princess. They cared greatly for their new friend and warned her not to answer the door to strangers while they were at work at the diamond mine.

The next day, an old woman came to the cottage and asked Snow White if she would like a wishing apple. She told Snow White that if she took a bite from the apple, her dreams would come true. The old woman was really the Queen in disguise, but Snow White did not know this. She bit the apple, wished for her prince, and fell into a deep sleep. She could only awaken with Love's First Kiss. The Seven Dwarfs chased the Queen and she fell from a cliff to her death.

The Seven Dwarfs placed Snow White in a coffin and kept vigil at her side. Time passed until the Prince, who had been searching for the maiden he had fallen in love with, found her. He kissed her and she awoke. The Prince and princess rode off to the Prince's castle, where they both lived happily ever after.

- 🍎 **Home:** The Queen's Castle
- 🍎 **Job:** Servant to the Queen
- 🍎 **Likes:** Singing, daydreaming, nature

Snow White

S now White is so beautiful that she is known as the fairest in the land. But Snow White is not only beautiful, she is kind and sweet-natured, too. She is also a wonderful story teller. Her favorite is about a prince and princess who fall in love.

Doing the housework all day is hard work and very dull, but Snow White never complains.

Songbird
If Snow White ever feels sad, she just sings a merry song and she immediately feels happy. Sometimes the birds tweet along too!

Daydream Believer
Hopeful Snow White spends her days dreaming of a happier future. She believes that one day a charming prince will rescue her from her wicked stepmother and they will fall in love.

"Everything is going to be all right."

Snow White sees nature in everything. Her dress is blue, like the sky, and yellow, like sunshine.

Cheerful Snow White spreads joy and happiness wherever she goes. A party is sure to cheer even the grumpiest of Dwarfs up!

Friendly Servant

Snow White's cruel stepmother always has a long list of duties for her stepdaughter to do. Hardworking Snow White sews, scrubs, and sweeps all day long. However, she is never lonely. Friendly Snow White has lots of animal friends who she sings and talks to.

With lips red as a rose, hair black as ebony, and skin white as snow, Snow White is declared the fairest in the land.

A HAPPY LIFE
Snow White knows that the best way to put a smile on your face is to have a song in your heart.

- **Home:** A little cottage
- **Job:** Digging diamonds
- **Favorite food:** Apple dumplings, gooseberry pie

The Seven Dwarfs

Meet the Seven Dwarfs! These seven little men are the hardest-working Dwarfs around. Even Sleepy, who is always napping, could never be called lazy. No wonder the Dwarfs' cottage is so messy: They are far too busy looking for diamonds to dust!

"Jiminy crickets!"

Doc

Sensible Doc is the leader of the gang. He has the very important job of checking the quality of each diamond that the Dwarfs mine.

Dopey

Dopey is the quietest Dwarf, but that's because he can't talk. At least he doesn't think he can—he's never actually tried!

Grumpy

Know-it-all Grumpy is really a softy at heart. Soon, even he can't help but be charmed by Snow White.

Happy

Happy is the happiest Dwarf in all the land. Not even the thought of having to wash before dinner can remove the smile from his face.

Sneezy

Sneezy's sneezes are so strong they can blow chairs and tables across the room. To stop him sneezing, the Dwarfs tie his beard under his nose!

Bashful

The smallest thing makes Bashful blush! He prefers to blend into the background. But being shy doesn't stop Bashful from batting his lashes at Snow White.

Off to Work

With a whistle and a song, the Seven Dwarfs march to work at the diamond mine where they dig, dig, dig for diamonds the whole day through. Every day is the same until one day, a pretty princess enters their lives.

Sleepy

Shhh! Taking a slumber is no problem for Sleepy. Sometimes, Sleepy yawns so widely, he catches houseflies in his mouth! He is usually too tired to notice though.

Housekeeping Hints

The sight of piles of dirty dishes, mountains of dust, and lots of washing is enough to send even the most patient of princesses into a state. But not Snow White—she's the Queen of housekeeping!

Enlist the help of your friends. If you work as a team, you are sure to get the job done twice as fast.

1 you are sure to get the job done twice as fast.

2 Work out each of your helpers' strong points.
For instance, deers' antlers make very useful hooks for hanging clean washing on.

3 Get your friends to lend a helping paw or tail.
Tongues can be used as sponges, but it is better to place dirty dishes in the tub!

4 A turtle's tummy has many surprising uses. As a washboard it helps remove the most stubborn of stains—even gooseberry pie!

5 Pretty flowers are a perfect way to brighten up even the darkest of rooms.

6 Whistle while you work! Chores won't take long when there's a song to help you on your way.

7 A broom is for sweeping up dust, not collecting it!

Made with Love

Snow White knows that a well-fed household is a happy household. She can bake everything from apple dumplings and plum pudding to gooseberry pie and scrumptious soup. Thoughtful Snow White adds a personal touch by putting the names of her friends on top of her pies to make them feel special.

The Queen

Behold the Queen! But beware—her icy stare is enough to strike terror through the heart of anyone. She is so scary that she is known throughout the land for her wicked ways. The jealous Queen will stop at nothing to fulfil her one ambition—to be the fairest in the land.

- **Home:** The Castle
- **Likes:** Giving orders, magic spells
- **Dislikes:** Pretty princesses

The Queen's Castle
With its creepy corridors, crowing crows, and spooky spiders, the Queen's castle matches her highness' dark personality perfectly. There's even a skeleton lurking in the dungeon!

THE PEDDLER'S DISGUISE SPELL

Handle with care! Just one drop of this powerful potion is enough to transform even the most regal Queen into the ugliest hag, warts and all.

Step I
A speck of mummy dust to make you old.

Step II
A little black of night to shroud clothes.

Step III
One old hag's cackle to age the voice.

Step IV
A shrill scream of fright to whiten the hair.

Step V
A big blast of wind to fan hate.

Step VI
A thunderbolt to mix it well.

Step VII
The transformation is complete.

The Huntsman

The Queen's Huntsman has always obeyed his orders. But unlike the Queen, he has a heart and doesn't agree with her wicked ways.

Vain Villain

When the vain Queen isn't gazing into her Magic Mirror or barking orders at Snow White, she is in her potion room concocting all manner of vile mixtures. She is a wicked witch and has many books on magic spells, from alchemy to sorcery, so it's best not to get on her bad side. But then again, the Queen doesn't have a good side!

The devious Queen's disguise is so brilliant that innocent Snow White thinks she is a harmless old woman and takes pity on her.

"Magic Mirror on the wall, who is the fairest one of all?"

- **Home:** Enchanted Forest
- **Favorite foods:** Nuts, berries, leaves
- **Like:** Their human friend, Snow White

Creature Companions

All creatures great and small want to be Snow White's friend. From chirruping birds and doe-eyed deer to cute chipmunks and bouncing bunnies, they are all drawn to Snow White's kind and gentle ways.

Friends Indeed

Cheerful Snow White has no problem making new friends. Surrounded by the curious creatures in the strange forest she is a little frightened, so she sings a song to cheer herself up. Soon, the forest is alive with the happy sound of singing and Snow White knows that she has made friends for life.

Perfect Pals

The forest birds know everyone in and around the forest. They want to do all they can to keep their new friend safe, and they know just the seven people who can help protect her.

The Prince

Charming, handsome, and caring—the Prince is simply perfect! He is all that any princess could ever wish for. The Prince is forever hopeful that one day he will find his one true love. Never did he think that a horse ride past the Queen's castle would lead to that dream coming true.

Home: A grand castle
Likes: Horse riding
Dream: To fall in love

Sweet Serenade

The Prince is a true romantic. He sings a love song to the pretty maiden in the castle, in the hope that he will win her heart forever.

True Love

The Prince always believed that he would find his one true love again. He is completely heartbroken when he finds Snow White in a coffin and kisses her farewell.

Happy Ending

With one kiss, the Prince makes all of Snow White's dreams come true. Just as she had wished, the charming Prince carries her away to his magnificent castle, where they live happily ever after.

Cinderella's Story

Once Upon a Time...

...there lived a father and his daughter, Cinderella. Cinderella's mother died when Cinderella was young. Her father wanted her to have a mother, so he married Lady Tremaine, who had two daughters—Anastasia and Drizella—and a cat named Lucifer. Cinderella's Stepmother and Stepsisters seemed nice at first. However, when Cinderella's father died, their cruel natures were revealed. They were so jealous of Cinderella's beauty that they forced her to be their servant.

One day, an invitation to a royal ball arrived. The King wanted his son, the Prince, to marry, and so he invited every maiden in the land to the ball. Anastasia, Drizella, and Cinderella were excited to meet the Prince, but Cinderella didn't have a dress to wear. So all her animal friends, including two mice called Jaq and Gus, made a gown for her out of Anastasia and Drizella's old dresses. When the jealous Stepsisters saw how pretty Cinderella looked, they tore her dress so she couldn't go to the ball.

Cinderella was very upset, but at that moment, her fairy godmother appeared. With a magic wand she turned a pumpkin into a carriage, mice into horses, Bruno the dog into a coach, and Major the horse into a coachman. She also used her wand to make a dress for Cinderella to wear, complete with glass slippers.  The Fairy Godmother told Cinderella that once the clock struck twelve, the spell would be broken and she would turn back into a servant.

As soon as the Prince saw Cinderella at the ball, he fell in love. Cinderella was enjoying herself so much that she forgot the time and in her rush to leave, she left one of her glass slippers on the castle stairs. The King demanded that every maiden must try on the slipper and the one whom it fitted would marry the Prince. When Lady Tremaine realized that Cinderella was the girl the Prince had fallen in love with, she locked Cinderella in her room. Luckily, Jaq and Gus got the key from Lady Tremaine's pocket and freed Cinderella. In one last attempt to ruin Cinderella's dream, Lady Tremaine tripped up the Duke, who was trying to find the owner of the slipper, and the slipper smashed into pieces. However, Cinderella had the other slipper, showing that she was the maiden the Prince loved. Cinderella and the Prince wed and lived happily ever after.

Job: Servant to her mean Stepmother

Greatest wish: To go to the royal ball

Favorite color: Blue

Cinderella

Charming Cinderella starts each new day with a smile on her face. Sometimes having to wake up early can be hard. However, with a little help from her animal friends, cheerful Cinderella is ready for the busy day ahead, forever hopeful that happiness is never far away.

Cool and Calm

Being a servant is often a balancing act. But no matter how much laundry she has to do and suppers she has to serve, Cinderella always remains calm.

Cinderella tries to see the good in everyone. She informs Bruno that everybody has good points, even Lady Tremaine's cat, Lucifer. Sometimes you just have to look a little harder to find them.

Courageous Cinderella

Lady Tremaine expects Cinderella to be seen and not heard. But with no one to stand up for her, Cinderella has learned to speak up for herself.

"It's like a dream. A wonderful dream come true."

Cinderella has a perfect view of the magnificent palace from her attic window. She hopes that one day soon she will get to visit it.

Cinderella's swept-up hairstyle makes her look elegant and graceful.

Blue silk matches Cinderella's sparkly eyes perfectly.

Secret Dream

She may have to work all day, but at night Cinderella dreams the most beautiful dream. When she awakens, she won't tell a soul what she has dreamed. Cinderella believes that if you speak about your dream, it won't come true.

SONG AND DANCE
Cinderella would love to go to a ball where she can dance and sing all night.

Home: Various nooks and crannies

Like: Making Cinderella smile and laugh

Dislike: Cruel cats

Animal Friends

No matter how busy Cinderella is, she always makes time for her assortment of animal friends. Loyal and brave, they brighten up her day. Not even the cruelest cat or the wickedest stepmother can stop them from spending time with their "Cinderelly."

Jaq and Gus

He might be small, but brave Jaq knows no fear when it comes to helping out his friends. New mouse on the block Gus isn't as mighty as Jaq but he has a huge heart—which is nearly as big as his appetite!

It takes a bit of teamwork and a lot of guts to outsmart Lady Tremaine. It also helps if you have a tough tail!

Mice Everywhere

The mice that live in the house often get together to think of ways to surprise Cinderella. After all, Cinderella makes sure they are all fed and clothed, so making a new dress or singing her a song is the least they can do for their favorite friend.

Cinderella is under strict orders to feed "His Majesty" Lucifer first. But she always makes sure that her pals get their fair share of food, too.

Bruno

Loyal bloodhound Bruno keeps Cinderella company when she is doing her chores. Bruno and fat cat Lucifer really do fight like cat and dog, and Bruno dreams of the day when he can get his claws into the crafty cat.

Bruno and Major never thought that one day they would get to take Cinderella to a royal ball!

Major

Major the horse has been Cinderella's firm friend since she was a little girl. He is getting old now, but his loyalty to Cinderella never fades.

Stepmother and Stepsisters

- *Home:* A faraway land
- *Like:* Telling Cinderella what to do
- *Dislike:* Cinderella

Since Cinderella's father died, her Stepmother and Stepsisters have done all they can to make Cinderella's life a misery. No trick is too wicked and no comment too nasty for this terrible trio. Meet the cruelest Stepmother and Stepsisters in the land!

"I never go back on my word."

Jealous Lady Tremaine will do anything to make sure Cinderella never finds happiness, even locking the poor girl in her room.

Lady Tremaine

Don't be fooled by Lady Tremaine's calm and composed appearance. Underneath the perfect hairdo is a cunning mind full of sinister tricks and scheming. She never raises her voice and she doesn't have to. Just one look from her is enough to send shivers down the spine.

Anastasia

Anastasia is mean, spoiled, and jealous of Cinderella's charm and beauty. She might try hard to look sweet but when she doesn't get her own way, she is a real grouch!

Drizella

Drizella loves to sleep in late, wants her supper to be served on time, and likes her laundry to be done every day. Luckily for her, she has Cinderella to wait on her.

Lady Tremaine demands self-control from everyone, especially her daughters. They try hard, but Anastasia and Drizella can't always carry it off. They hope to be like their dear mother one day though.

Pampered Pet

Fat cat Lucifer is as spoiled by Lady Tremaine as Anastasia and Drizella are. He is the first to get fed, and he has his own luxurious bed. Lazy Lucifer doesn't hurry for anyone, except when there's a mouse in the house. The only things Lucifer hates more than mice are baths!

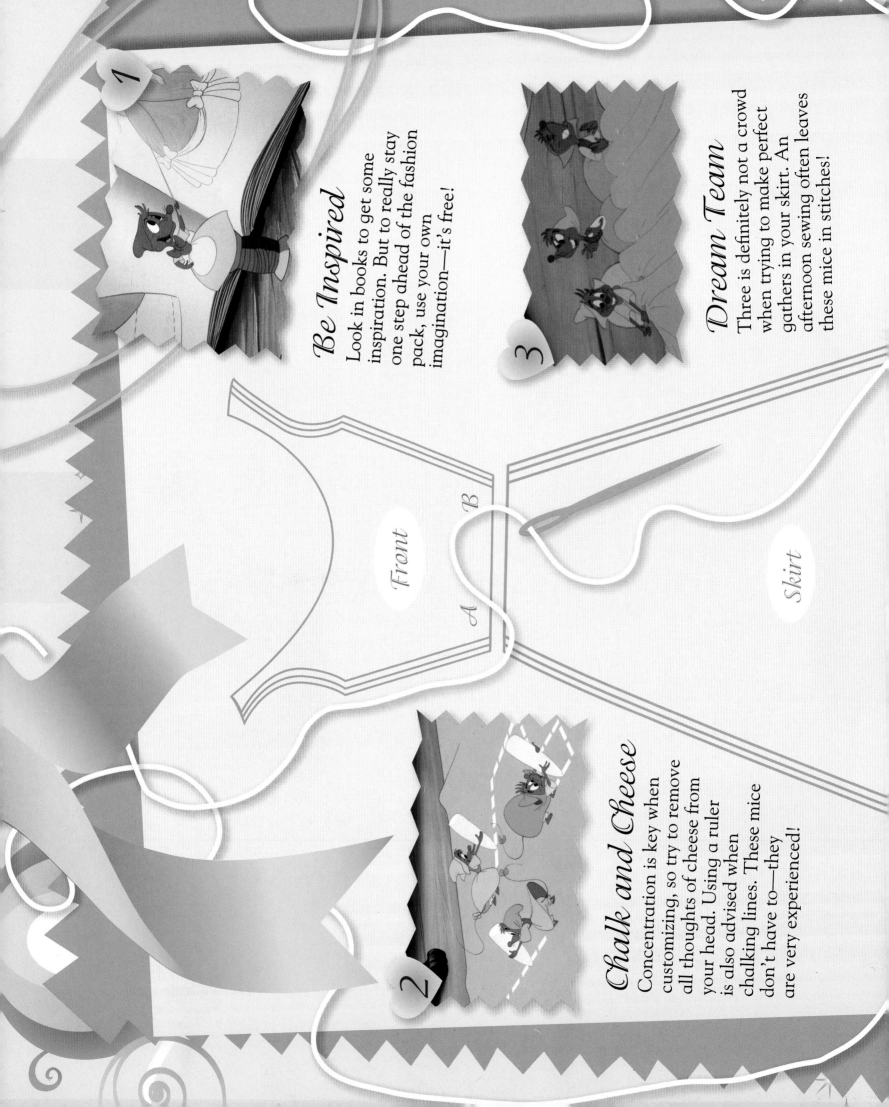

Be Inspired

Look in books to get some inspiration. But to really stay one step ahead of the fashion pack, use your own imagination—it's free!

Dream Team

Three is definitely not a crowd when trying to make perfect gathers in your skirt. An afternoon sewing often leaves these mice in stitches!

Chalk and Cheese

Concentration is key when customizing, so try to remove all thoughts of cheese from your head. Using a ruler is also advised when chalking lines. These mice don't have to—they are very experienced!

Front

Skirt

A

B

Fabulous Fashion

To ensure you stay a cut above the rest, follow the lead of Cinderella's mice pals and get ready for some cool customization. Take one old dress, add a snippet of imagination, a bit of teamwork, and a needle and thread, of course.

Perfect Hem

A straight hemline is the quickest way to achieving a professional finish, so be sure to take extra care when measuring a skirt.

Beautiful Bow

A bow made from silk ribbon adds a pretty touch to any dress. These mice find it helps to have some bird buddies to lend a helping beak.

Pretty Dress

With a couple of finishing touches, like some beads, a headband, and a dazzling smile, Cinderella has a dress fit for a princess!

Fairy Godmother

The Fairy Godmother really is extraordinary. She appears as if by magic, ready to wave her wand (once she has found it), and make wishes come true. Her one and only rule is that you have to believe in your dreams.

Likes: Making people happy with magic

Dislikes: Losing her magic wand

Favorite spell: She can't remember!

"On the stroke of twelve, the spell will be broken…"

Rags to Riches

The Fairy Godmother knows many spells and is also incredibly wise. She sets to work making Cinderella look as pretty as a princess, but warns her that even dreams cannot last forever.

After a few magic words and lots of fairy dust, the transformation is complete. Cinderella *will* go to the ball!

Cinderella's Coach

Only the Fairy Godmother could see the potential of a pumpkin. She knows that no princess worth her slippers would ever turn up to a royal ball on foot.

Prince Charming

Prince Charming lives a truly charmed life. He has a loving father and grew up in a magnificent castle. He doesn't expect to fall in love with any of the maidens who queue up to meet him, but magic is in the air!

Home: The castle
Likes: Dancing a romantic waltz
Dislikes: Meeting many maidens

Every maiden in the land wants to be the one who the prince falls in love with, including Cinderella's ugly Stepsisters. But Prince Charming only has eyes for one.

Handsome Stranger

Prince Charming has always dreamed of falling in love. Even though he doesn't know the maiden's name, he knows he has found his one true love! As they dance, it feels as if they are the only ones in the room.

Spellbound

From deep sleeps and beastly beasts, to fabulous frocks and slimy frogs, baddies and goodies alike are all experts in the art of spells. A wave of a wand or a drop of vile potion can achieve all sorts of weird and wonderful magic. These princes and princesses have all been touched by a little bit of magic that has transformed their lives forever.

What do you get when you take one singing mermaid and one sea witch on a mission to take over Atlantica? A dream come true! At last Ariel gets her sea legs and becomes a human.

Being green and slimy with four legs is just not Naveen's style. But being a frog does have its good points, like having an extra-long tongue to catch yummy flies with.

The prince might be handsome but he is selfish. It is a hard lesson that the enchantress teaches the prince. Being a big hairy Beast is no fun at all, when everyone is scared of you.

Aurora's family is worried when Maleficent arrived at Aurora's birth celebration, but sometimes good can come from bad. Maleficent's wicked spell puts Aurora into the deepest sleep of her life, but it is worth it—she wakes up to Prince Phillip and this time she's not dreaming!

Take one fairy godmother and one servant with a dream. Add a sprinkling of fairy dust and a dash of magic words. A twirl for luck and Cinderella is ready for the royal ball!

Aurora's Story

Once Upon a Time...

...a princess named Aurora was born to King Stefan and Queen Leah. Friendly fairies Flora, Fauna, and Merryweather blessed Aurora with the gifts of beauty and song. But a wicked fairy, Maleficent, cursed the princess: Before the sun set on her sixteenth birthday, Aurora would prick her finger on the spindle of a spinning wheel and die!

Merryweather was able to change the curse of death to the gift of life. If Aurora did prick her finger she would fall into a deep sleep and only True Love's Kiss would wake her. To protect Aurora, the fairies planned to disguise themselves as peasant women and raise Aurora as Briar Rose, in a forest cottage. To keep

the location a secret, they wouldn't use magic or allow Briar Rose to talk to strangers. Even the princess would not know who she truly was.

Briar Rose grew to be gentle and kind, but she was lonely. One day, Briar Rose met a young man in the forest. She didn't know his name, but she loved him at once.

While Briar Rose was in the forest, the fairies were preparing for her return to the castle. They also wanted to make her a dress and a cake for her sixteenth birthday, but they had to use magic. Maleficent's raven spy saw the fairy dust fly out of the chimney and told Maleficent.

Briar Rose returned to the cottage and told the fairies about the man she had met. They finally revealed that she was a princess and due to marry Prince Phillip, who she had met as a baby. She could never see her new friend again!

The fairies led the heartbroken Aurora to the castle where her parents, Prince Phillip, and Prince Phillip's father, King Stefan, were awaiting her return. Prince Phillip didn't realize that the girl he had met in the forest and fallen in love with was actually Princess Aurora. But before he discovered the truth, Maleficent worked her evil magic on Aurora: Before the sun set, Aurora had touched the spindle and fallen into a deep sleep.

Suddenly, the fairies realized that Aurora's love from the forest was actually Prince Phillip! They helped him escape Maleficent and find the princess. With True Love's Kiss, Aurora awoke. How happy she was to see her dream prince and live her dream.

- 👑 **Favorite color:** Pink
- 👑 **Likes:** Singing, daydreaming, walks in the forest
- 👑 **Dislikes:** Being treated like a child, feeling lonely

Aurora

Gentle and kind, Princess Aurora is beautiful both on the inside and the outside. Her dreams and sweet songs are filled with love and romance. As Briar Rose, she works hard at her duties and always does what is asked of her.

"If you dream a thing more than once, it's sure to come true."

Royal Family

King Stefan and Queen Leah had always wished for a child of their own. When baby Aurora was born, they loved her at once! The proud parents were heartbroken at having to give their beloved daughter to the kind fairies. But they knew that she would be well looked after.

Briar Rose's lovely singing voice makes for pretty songs with her feathered friends. They chirp along as she sings about her dream of meeting someone to love.

ANIMAL FRIENDS

When Briar Rose feels lonely, she turns to the playful birds, squirrels, and her other furry friends for company.

Flora's gift of golden hair and rose-red lips makes Princess Aurora a rare beauty.

Mother Hens

Briar Rose always listens to Flora, Fauna, and Merryweather, even though they sometimes treat her like a child. The fairies are like mothers to Briar Rose.

Sweet Sixteen

Even in her humble forest home, Briar Rose's grace and kindness always shone through. But when she takes her place as Princess Aurora on her sixteenth birthday, royal robes give her a whole new sparkle!

Dream Prince

Briar Rose always believed that love would find her. The handsome stranger she meets in the forest is like a dream come true!

Aurora's dress was made by magic— when Flora gave up on sewing it by hand!

Home: A cottage in the forest

Like: Briar Rose, magic, happy endings

Dislike: Maleficent, saying goodbye to Briar Rose

Flora, Fauna, and Merryweather

The three fairies, Flora, Fauna, and Merryweather, are good and kind, and clever and brave. With a flick of their wands and a sprinkle of fairy dust, they make magic that brings joy and happiness. But out of love for Princess Aurora, they do their greatest trick of all: Live without magic.

Fauna

Good-natured Fauna sees the positive side of everyone—she thinks that even Maleficent can't be all bad. With her talent for magic, she blesses the infant Aurora with the gift of song. But what she has always wanted to do is make a cake!

"Each of us the child may bless, with a single gift, no more, no less."

Fauna and the other fairies can make themselves tiny in order to fly.

A New Look

To help Princess Aurora, the fairies trade in their wands and wings for simple dresses and aprons, as part of their disguise as peasant women.

Flora blesses the infant Aurora with the gift of beauty.

Magical Mischief

When the fairies have a disagreement over the color of Aurora's new dress, their magical fight changes Merryweather's outfit, too!

Flora

As the leader of the fairies, it is Flora who comes up with the plan to raise Aurora far away from the castle. She loves flowery pink, which she uses in the dress she makes for Aurora's sixteenth birthday celebration.

Merryweather is the smallest of the three fairies, but she can be as stubborn as someone twice her size!

Merryweather

Quick-thinking Merryweather weakens Maleficent's curse as her gift to Aurora. Merryweather is practical and levelheaded, but she is also loving, romantic, and brave.

Fearless Fairies

Although much smaller than Maleficent, her trolls, or even her raven, the fairies boldly help Prince Phillip escape the Forbidden Mountain. Merryweather even turns the raven to stone!

The best gift of all is from Merryweather: A gentle sleeping spell to take the sting out of Maleficent's curse.

What a pretty package! Rose-red lips and golden hair are Flora's gifts to the baby princess.

A talent for music makes a thoughtful present from Fauna for the princess who has everything.

This birthday cake is made with love—but the melty, gooey mess isn't quite what Fauna intended!

Flora's handmade party dress isn't up to palace standards, but it is the thought that counts!

Fairies' Gift Guide

Aurora has three very special friends in Flora, Fauna, and Merryweather. They love to treat the princess with unusual gifts—some more unusual than others!

- **Home:** The Forbidden Mountain
- **Likes:** Power, her raven
- **Dislikes:** Stupidity, being ignored

Maleficent

On the Forbidden Mountain Maleficent, the most powerful and wicked of all the fairies, rules over an army of monsters. Mean Maleficent knows all about terror and revenge—but nothing of love.

At Aurora's birth celebration, Maleficent pretends to be gracious, but then frightens everyone with a curse: When Aurora turns sixteen, she will prick her finger on a spindle and die!

Terrible Trolls

They're mean and menacing, but Maleficent's goons are anything but clever. They waste years searching for a baby instead of a growing princess!

The Raven

Maleficent usually keeps her loyal pet nearby, but she also relies on his wits and wings to run important errands.

Maleficent wears flowing robes in dark and gloomy purple and black.

This staff is topped by a magical orb, which swirls and glows when Maleficent casts her spells.

"I really felt quite distressed at not receiving an invitation."

Wicked Witch

An angry Maleficent is a scary sight! When the king and queen don't invite her to Aurora's birth celebration, they learn that the "mistress of all evil" is unforgiving. She'll do anything for revenge, including casting terrible curses with her magical orb.

The Dragon

Maleficent changes into a giant, fire-breathing dragon to fight Prince Phillip. With the help of the good fairies, Phillip uses the Sword of Truth to defeat the beast—and conquer Maleficent!

- **Home:** The forest
- **Favorite foods:** Nuts, berries, leaves
- **Like:** Listening to stories, singing, playing with Briar Rose

Forest Friends

With no human friends to keep her company, Briar Rose turns to the feathered and furry creatures in the forest. They adore the gentle Briar Rose, and hurry to her side when she goes into the forest to walk or pick berries.

Good Listeners

Briar Rose can't help but wonder: Why does each bird have a partner to sing to, but she does not? Luckily, she does have lots of animal friends in the forest who listen to her worries and daydreams.

Song and Dance

When the animals find Phillip's clothes, they dress up as Briar Rose's "dream prince!" The playful creatures do their best to make Briar Rose happy, even if it is just for a moment.

Prince Phillip

Adventurous Phillip loves galloping through the forest, and he can wield a sword with great skill. But the bold prince is really a romantic at heart! He believes in love at first sight—and when he does find love he is determined to hold onto it.

- **Home:** His father, King Hubert's castle
- **Likes:** Horseback riding, music
- **Dream:** To fall in love

Happy Couple

Together at last! Princess Aurora and Prince Phillip can leave danger and mystery behind, and focus on their happily ever after.

Thanks to the good fairies, Phillip carries the Shield of Virtue and the Sword of Truth.

To the Rescue

Riding his faithful horse Samson, Phillip must escape Maleficent's trolls, falling boulders, flying arrows, a forest of thorns, and the dragon before he can reach his beloved Aurora.

Fighting for Love

The prince needs all his courage to get back to his Sleeping Beauty. But when true love is at stake, brave Phillip will take on any challenge—even the fearsome dragon!

Ariel's Story

Once Upon a Time...

...in the underwater city of Atlantica, there lived a little mermaid named Ariel. Her father, King Triton, had forbidden the merpeople from any contact with humans, but Ariel really wanted to be human. One day, Ariel swam up to a ship's porthole and fell in love with a human, Prince Eric. There was a terrible storm and Ariel saved Eric's life. When Eric awoke, all he could remember about Ariel was her beautiful voice. He was determined to find the girl who had saved his life and marry her.

Ariel's father was very angry that Ariel had disobeyed him, and ordered Sebastian the crab to watch over her. Meanwhile, the banished sea witch Ursula sent her eel spies, Flotsam and Jetsam, to convince Ariel that Ursula could make her dream of being human come true. Desperate to see her prince again, Ariel went to visit Ursula. She told Ariel she could make her human for three days in exchange for Ariel's voice. Ariel would have to make Prince Eric fall in love with her and give her the kiss of true love before the sun set on the third day. If Ariel succeeded, she would remain human forever. If she failed, she would return to her mermaid form and belong to Ursula. To be with her love, Ariel signed over her voice. Ursula took Ariel's voice and kept it in a shell around her neck and promptly changed Ariel into a human.

*E*ven without her voice, Ariel almost made Eric fall in love with her. However, before he could kiss Ariel, Ursula disguised herself as a woman named Vanessa. When Eric heard her voice, which was really Ariel's, he believed that Vanessa was his love, and promised to marry Vanessa.

*L*uckily, Ariel's seagull friend, Scuttle, discovered that Vanessa was Ursula in disguise. He and his friends stopped the wedding and broke Ursula's shell. Ariel got her voice back and the spell on Eric was broken. When Eric heard Ariel's voice he realized that she was the girl who had saved him, but the sun had set. Ariel and Ursula turned back into their original forms and Ursula offered to exchange Ariel for King Triton. Ursula turned the king into a sea creature and became Queen of Atlantica. Ursula tried to kill Eric, but instead destroyed Flotsam and Jetsam. She then tried to kill Ariel, but Eric saved her and killed Ursula. Finally, King Triton returned to his merman form. When he saw how much Ariel and Eric loved each other, he changed Ariel into a human so that they could both live happily ever after, on dry land.

- **Home:** Atlantica
- **Hobbies:** Exploring sea ruins
- **Favorite human object:** A "dinglehopper" to help style your hair

Ariel

Adventurous Ariel dreams of being human so she can dance on dry land and do everything that humans do. Ariel is always searching for her next big adventure—as long as it involves danger and excitement, she's there!

Ariel has a cave full of human objects that she and her friends have collected on their adventures. She thinks that a world with so many amazing things must be wonderful.

Ariel is a true romantic. Nothing will stop her listening to her heart.

Human Hope

Ariel thinks there must be more to life than what Atlantica has to offer. There is a big world outside of the ocean and she wants to be part of it. However, Ariel's father, King Triton, sees things differently to his youngest daughter and forbids her to have anything to do with dangerous humans. But Ariel will do anything to make her dreams come true.

"Some day I'll be part of your world."

The salt in the sea gives Ariel's locks a beautiful wave.

Lovesick

The first human Ariel sees up close is Prince Eric, on his ship. He is dancing and having fun, and Ariel falls for him hook, line, and sinker.

Fearless Fish

Ariel is both bold and brave, and not much scares her. When she sees that the handsome stranger from the ship is in danger, she doesn't think twice about saving him from drowning.

Beautiful Voice

She is the little mermaid with the big voice. But sometimes Ariel would much rather explore creepy sea ruins than sing at one of Atlantica's concerts.

UNDER THE SEA

Once, Ariel and Flounder were exploring a sea ruin and they were chased by a scary shark!

- **Home:** Underwater palace
- **Like:** Organizing lavish music concerts
- **Dislike:** Fishing nets

Ariel's Family

The beautiful undersea palace in Atlantica is home to Ariel, her six sisters, and their strict but caring father, King Triton, who is ruler of the merpeople. Ariel is the baby of the family, but she wishes they would see that she is now all grown-up.

King Triton

Ariel's father believes that all humans are bad and contact with them is forbidden. The easiest way to make King Triton angry is by disobeying him. When he loses his temper, the whole of Atlantica knows about it.

Letting Go

King Triton realizes that his little mermaid is not so little anymore. The time has finally come for Ariel to stand on her own two feet.

Ariel's Sisters

Aquata, Andrina, Arista, Attina, Adella, and Alana enjoy searching for oyster pearls to decorate their hair and sharing makeup tips. But Ariel's all-singing, all-dancing sisters are happiest when they are performing in one of Atlantica's many concerts.

Prince Eric

Prince Eric loves everything to do with the sea and he even has his own ship. He is a great catch and the whole Kingdom wants to see him married. Eric knows the girl of his dreams is out there somewhere— he just didn't expect her to be a mermaid!

Best friend: Max, his dog
Favorite place: His ship
Likes: Taking Max for long walks on the beach

"You're the one I've been looking for."

Tricked
Disguised as Vanessa, Ursula uses Ariel's voice to make Eric believe that she is the girl who saved his life.

Ship's Crew
Easygoing Eric gets on with everyone, especially his manservant, Grimsby. Eric's crew is certainly a happy one.

True Romance
Prince Eric lost his dream girl once, and he wasn't going to lose her again. He bravely uses his sailing skills to defeat the evil sea witch, Ursula, and save Ariel.

51

- Favorite food: Anything tasty from the sea
- Like: Adventures, writing music, flying
- Dislike: Wicked tentacled sea creatures

Ariel's Friends

Meet Ariel's friends! Whether she needs some company on one of her adventures, advice on how to catch a prince, or just wants to know what a strange human object is, Ariel's loyal group of pals are always willing to help.

Flounder

Faithful friend Flounder is Ariel's loyal companion on her adventures. He is timid and tiny, but that doesn't stop him from sticking up for his best pal when their adventures get them into trouble.

Scaredy-fish

Flounder's biggest fear is sharks. Unfortunately, living in the sea he doesn't have to swim far to see one.

Flounder knows that the surest way to put a smile on his best friends' face is with a new human object to add to her collection.

Sebastian

Horatio Thelonious Ignatius Crustaceous Sebastian (Sebastian for short) is Atlantica's finest court composer. Sebastian is never lost for words and can talk himself out of—and into—any situation. He loves his underwater life and doesn't understand why anyone would want to live on dry land.

Sebastian is more used to writing symphonies than looking after mermaids. Soon the crabby crab shows he's not as hard as his shell and agrees to help Ariel fulfil her dream.

"I'll try to help you find that Prince."

Scuttle

Scatty seagull Scuttle likes to think he is the bird with the big brain when it comes to anything human. He is always Ariel's first port of call when she needs one of her precious human objects to be identified.

Scuttle is never wrong about anything—at least not when it's important. He knows a sea witch in disguise when he sees one, and warns Ariel that Ursula is up to no good.

Ursula

Sneaky sea witch Ursula may deal in dreams, but she is every mermaid's worst nightmare. She will smile at you, listen to your tale of woe, and lend you a helping tentacle—but only if the price is right, or course.

- **Likes:** Plotting revenge on King Triton
- **Dislikes:** Time wasters
- **Favorite food:** Anything living and breathing

Flotsam and Jetsam
Ursula loves her "poopsies" to death. Her pet eels slither around Atlantica, spying on the merfolk for their mistress.

Sea Witch
Banished from Atlantica by King Triton, Ursula now lurks in the depths of the ocean. She has made a business out of making the merfolk of Atlantica's dreams come true. But sneaky Ursula has her own dream—to get revenge on King Triton for banishing her and become Queen of Atlantica.

Ursula persuades Ariel to sign over her precious voice, in exchange for making her human. But Ursula has bigger fish to fry—and Ariel is the fastest way to realizing her ambition.

Smiling Sea Witch

Ursula's grin and fake charm is usually enough to get the merfolk to sign over their most prized possessions.

Ursula's Makeup Regime

1. Clams aren't just for eating. Used as lipstick, clam juice makes the perfect pout.

2. A squirt of mousse can make your hair as big as your personality.

3. Use crushed seaweed to shadow the eyes and make merfolk green with envy.

4. Finally, add a dot of squid ink for a beauty spot.

Devious Disguise

From dreams to disguises, the sly sea witch's magical powers are legendary. She takes matters into her own tentacles when she discovers that Eric has fallen for Ariel. But even disguised as Vanessa, Ursula's magic powers can't hide the evil glint in her eye—which is pure Ursula.

"I always was a girl with an eye for a bargain."

Ariel's Collection

Ariel has a secret hobby—collecting all things from the human world. Hidden away in her secret cavern, Ariel keeps her impressive treasure trove of gadgets and gizmos, and trinkets and "thingamabobs" that she has collected since she was young. Ariel might not know what each item is called, but each of her precious objects gives Ariel a connection to the human world she longs to be a part of. Come inside and explore Ariel's amazing collection.

This clown-faced toy always pops up at the worst times. Ariel hasn't worked out how to stop it!

Scuttle says this object is a "snarfblat," invented by humans to make music with when they are bored.

This happy couple dance round and round to the pretty music. Ariel dreams of being human so she can do the same.

Ariel thinks this pretty ornament is very handy for storing her "dinglehopper," which is used to comb hair according to Scuttle.

Ariel displays her ornaments and clocks on shelves so that her cavern doesn't get too cluttered.

Pearls are usually found in oysters, but Ariel keeps her precious pearls in this treasure chest.

This statue of Eric was a gift from Flounder. Ariel doesn't think it is as handsome as the real thing though.

Cinderella believes that if you tell someone your wish, it won't come true. She doesn't tell a soul, and, sure enough, Prince Charming waltzes into her life.

Aurora's dream of a handsome prince always seemed so real. Now her real life seems like a perfect dream!

Wishing and Dreaming

*E*very princess has a dream or a wish that they hold in their hearts. Some keep their dreams secret, while others tell people close to them. But all the princesses want more than anything for their dreams to come true.

Tiana is so desperate to own a restaurant that she wishes on the Evening Star. But she knows that wishing is not enough—she will have to work hard, too.

Jasmine doesn't need a genie to make her wishes come true. She believes in herself and knows that one day she will be able to make her own choices.

Pocahontas believed her dream of a spinning arrow meant something exciting would happen. She never thought the arrow would point to love.

Belle's Story

Once Upon a Time...

...there was a young girl named Belle. She lived in a small town with her father Maurice, an inventor. An arrogant hunter, Gaston, was determined to make Belle his bride, but she did not want to marry him.

One day, Belle's father rode off to show his inventions at a Fair, but he became lost in the woods. His horse, Philippe, ran away and Maurice had to seek shelter at a dark castle. The castle seemed to be deserted, but Maurice found that many of the household objects, including a candelabra named Lumiere and a clock named Cogsworth, could talk! Just as Maurice was getting used to his strange surroundings, he came face to face with the castle's terrifying occupant—the Beast. The Beast was in fact a prince, but an enchantress had placed a spell on him to teach him a lesson. The Beast hid himself away. His only window to the outside world was his magic mirror.

The Beast believed that Maurice had come to stare at him, and locked the poor man in his tower. When Philippe returned home alone, a worried Belle set off in search of her father. She soon discovered that he was the Beast's prisoner, and offered to take his place. Although she feared him at first, Belle grew closer to the Beast and began to care for him.

Over time, the Beast fell in love with Belle, but he knew that she missed her father. In an act of true love, the Beast allowed Belle to leave the castle. She took the magic mirror with her to remember him by. However, when Belle arrived home, she found that her father was about to be taken to a lunatic asylum. No one believed Maurice's tales of the Beast and Gaston had concocted a plan with the asylum owner, Monsieur D'Arque, that would force Belle to marry him. Belle proved that the Beast was real by showing them the Beast in the magic mirror, and saved her father. But Gaston and his friend LeFou had persuaded the townsfolk to hunt and kill the Beast.

The Beast was so sad and lonely without Belle that he did not want to fight. However, his loyal servants made sure that the townsfolk did not get very far! Belle rushed to save the Beast. When the Beast saw that Belle had come back to him, he defeated Gaston. The kind Beast spared Gaston's life but the cowardly hunter sneaked up and dealt him one last blow. As the Beast lay dying, Belle confessed her love to him. The Beast returned to his human form and, after Belle realized that this handsome prince was indeed her beloved Beast, the pair lived happily ever after.

- **Home**: The edge of a small town in France
- **Likes**: Reading wonderful stories and dreaming of adventures
- **Dislikes**: Arrogant people, like Gaston

Belle

Most people agree that Belle is beautiful but a little strange. They cannot understand why she spends her time reading books and won't marry Gaston, the handsomest man in town. Little do they know that Belle dreams of a very different life for herself, far away from her small town.

"Everything's going to be fine—you'll see."

Bookish Beauty

Belle longs to visit the faraway places she reads about in books and she would love to have someone to share her dreams with. But she could never marry a man like Gaston: Belle's head may be in the clouds, but her feet are on solid ground.

Maurice

Belle's father Maurice is always creating crazy new machines. Most of his inventions do not actually work, but Belle is sure he will be successful one day.

Even in her wildest dreams, Belle never imagined that she would become a princess!

Patient Friend

It doesn't take Belle long to discover the Beast is not nearly as terrifying as he looks. Belle also teaches him to read, so that he can share her passion for books.

Belle's favorite color is yellow. This fabulous gown reminds her of a beautiful sunny day.

Brave Belle

Belle would do anything for the people she loves. She bravely rescues her father and when the Beast is in danger, Belle rushes to his side.

Happy Ending

Belle's love for the Beast sets him free from the enchantress's spell, and it changes her life too. She has a huge library of her own, full of books to read! But best of all, she has someone to share her dreams with.

Super Stories

Belle has a colorful imagination. She likes to imagine visiting all the exotic places that she reads about in her favorite books.

The Beast

The Beast is so used to being alone that he doesn't know how to behave around Belle. His servants tell him to act nice, but he is more comfortable with being scary. However, as the Beast gets to know Belle his true character begins to emerge. He even makes Belle laugh!

- **Home**: A huge enchanted castle
- **Dislikes**: His appearance, being stared at
- **Needs**: To find true love and break the enchantress's spell

The Beast is ashamed of the way he looks. He imagines that people will make fun of him, so he hides inside his gloomy castle, with only his magic mirror to view the world from.

Spellbound

The Beast used to be a handsome but selfish prince. One day a beggar woman asked him to give her shelter in exchange for a rose. He refused, so after warning him not to judge by appearances, the woman transformed into a beautiful enchantress. She put a magic spell on the prince and his castle.

If the prince could not learn to love and find someone to love him back by the time the last petal on the enchanted rose fell, he would have to remain a Beast forever.

Being Beastly

Maurice is terrified of the angry Beast. However, when Belle takes her father's place she learns that beneath his fierce exterior, the Beast is gentle and thoughtful.

Although the Beast looks terrifying, Belle can see the kindness and love in his eyes.

"*You've come to stare at the Beast, haven't you?*"

Soulmates

When the Beast allows Belle to return home to her father, he proves that he is no longer selfish. Although he longs to break the enchantress's curse, he loves Belle too much to see her unhappy. Fortunately for the Beast, Belle loves him too and is able to break the spell, just in time.

At first Belle doesn't recognize the handsome man standing in front of her. But after gazing into his eyes, she can see that he is her same beloved Beast.

The Beast won't miss having huge claws and a tail now that he is human.

Lumiere

The Beast's friendly butler, Lumiere, has lots of advice for the Beast on the best way to win Belle's heart. He also falls in love with the Featherduster.

Lumiere is pleased to return to his good-looking human form. Now he can have a girl on each arm!

The Servants

The Beast isn't the only one in the castle who is under a spell. The enchantress's magic turns all the servants into household objects and unless the Beast can find true love, everyone will stay that way forever. The servants are determined to help the Beast win Belle's heart so they can return to their rightful forms.

Cogsworth

Cogsworth

Clever clock Cogsworth is the head of the Beast's household. He is an expert on the history of the Beast's castle and he takes his job very seriously.

Cogsworth is much more uptight than his laidback friend Lumiere. He likes everything to run smoothly and on time—anything to avoid upsetting the Beast!

Footstool

The Beast's pet dog doesn't really mind life as a footstool. After all, he still has a tail to wag. But nothing beats a game of "fetch!" in the garden with his pal Chip.

Featherduster

The Featherduster has plenty of work to do keeping the huge castle clean and tidy. Although she is fond of the smooth-talking Lumiere, she is careful not to get burnt by the charming candelabra.

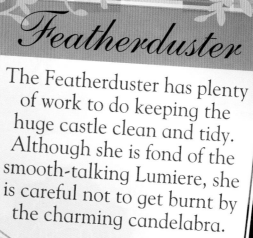

Wardrobe

The castle's resident opera singer finds life as a wardrobe pretty dull—until Belle arrives. She loves dressing Belle in beautiful outfits, and thinks that the young girl was brave to take her father's place in the castle.

Mrs. Potts and Chip

It is not always easy for an enchanted teapot to run the castle's kitchen, but Mrs. Potts does her best. The Beast's cook combines her work with looking after her family, including her youngest son, Chip. Mrs. Potts and Chip think Belle is wonderful and will do anything they can to help the Beast win her love.

Chip secretly travels with Belle when she goes home. He uses one of Maurice's inventions to free Belle and her father.

Life is much easier for Mrs. Potts and Chip when they are not made of china. The Beast's castle will be a happy place to live.

Gaston

Gaston the hunter is not only the handsomest man in town, he is also the vainest. He loves gazing at himself in the mirror and believes that Belle is the only girl in town (almost) as good looking as he is. Gaston is determined to marry her—whether she wants to or not.

"This is the day your dreams come true!"

Gaston has the biggest muscles in town and the biggest ego. He is the local hero and all the townspeople admire him.

Hunting for a Wife

Gaston thinks that Belle is a little odd for reading books with no pictures in them, but she is beautiful. Arrogant Gaston always gets what he wants and he will marry Belle, by any means necessary. How could any girl possibly resist the great Gaston? It is unthinkable! Not that Gaston wastes much time thinking...

Monsieur D'Arque

Asylum owner Monsieur D'Arque pretends to be shocked at Gaston's wicked plan to imprison Belle's father, but really all he cares about is money. Greedy Monsieur D'Arque would do just about anything to make a quick buck!

LeFou

Loyal LeFou is always ready to do whatever it takes to help his friend out. Although Gaston is often mean to him, LeFou thinks that Gaston is the greatest. He would love to be as handsome and popular as Gaston and believes that Belle should feel honored to be chosen as Gaston's bride.

When Gaston's wedding day dawns, he hasn't even asked Belle to marry him yet! He has no doubt that Belle will say "yes" and that they will have six or seven children together.

A Beastly End

When the kindhearted Beast spares Gaston's life, the hunter reveals his true cowardly nature and attacks the Beast. Although the Beast is badly hurt, it is Gaston who falls to his death.

B. Rose

Bedtime Stories

In Belle's opinion, the best books are about far-off places, and contain swordfights, magic spells, and—of course—a prince in disguise.

C. LaBouff

Princess Tales

Rags to Riches

People like Gaston don't really understand why Belle likes books so much. Belle believes that Gaston would be a much nicer person if he spent more time reading, and less time looking in the mirror!

S. White

Books aren't just full of great stories, you can also learn a lot from them. By reading books, Belle has learned all about many different subject, from astronomy to zebras.

Mrs. Potts

Time for Tea

In books, Belle can have the life she has always dreamed of. She has read all the books in her local bookshop at least once.

Belle's favorite part of the story is when the heroine meets Prince Charming but doesn't realize who he is until Chapter Three. If only real life could be like that!

Belle's Books

Belle might not have got her wish to see the world, but she has found the next best thing—reading about it in books! With a little imagination, a good book can take the reader on the most wonderful adventures.

Jasmine's Story

Once Upon a Time...

...in Agrabah there lived a beautiful Sultan's daughter named Jasmine. According to the laws of her country, Jasmine must marry a prince before her next birthday. Unfortunately, that was in three days and Jasmine kept on sending her suitors away!

One night, Jasmine sneaked out of the palace, with a little help from her pet tiger, Rajah. Covering her head so that no one would recognize her, she went to the  marketplace. When she saw a hungry child, Jasmine took an apple from a stall and gave it to him. The stall owner thought she was a thief, but a street urchin named Aladdin, and his pet monkey Abu, came to her rescue.

The Sultan's evil vizier, Jafar, needed Aladdin's help with a secret task, so he sent his guards to arrest Aladdin. Jasmine revealed her true identity to save her new friend, but the guards still took him away.

Jafar told Jasmine that Aladdin was dead, but in fact he had sent him to the Cave of Wonders to find a magic lamp. Aladdin found the lamp, but the evil Jafar tried to kill him. With some help from Abu and a Magic Carpet, Aladdin escaped and discovered that the lamp contained a powerful genie. The Genie granted Aladdin three wishes. Aladdin used the first one to transform himself into Prince Ali Ababwa and set off to woo Princess Jasmine.

At first, Jasmine was not impressed with the confident Prince Ali, but she soon discovered that he shared some remarkable similarities with her friend from the marketplace. After an amazing magic carpet ride, Jasmine was convinced that she had found a real prince at last and could not wait to tell her father.

However, Jafar's parrot, Iago, stole the magic lamp from Aladdin, and Jafar used the Genie's magic to become the Sultan. He made the Sultan a jester, and forced Jasmine to be a servant. He also revealed that Aladdin was not really a prince and banished him from the country. Jafar used his second wish to become the most powerful sorcerer in the world, but Aladdin returned on the Magic Carpet and convinced Jafar to use his final wish to become a genie. With Jafar trapped inside the lamp forever, Aladdin used his own third wish to free the Genie from the lamp. The Sultan changed the law so that Jasmine could marry whoever she chose. And of course, Jasmine chose Aladdin.

Jasmine

Jasmine appears to have everything a girl could possibly want—she lives in a luxurious palace, has lots of fine clothes, and even owns a pet tiger. However, the beautiful princess feels trapped and knows nothing of the world outside the palace. She longs to be free to make her own choices.

♥ *Home:* A magnificent palace at Agrabah

♥ *Likes:* Adventure, seeing the world

♥ *Dislikes:* Being told what to do all the time

"I am not a prize to be won!"

Jasmine has never left the palace, so she decides to sneak out. There's a big world out there and she is determined to see some of it!

Best Friend

Life can be very lonely for Jasmine and her only friend is Rajah, a tiger. Rajah is a sympathetic listener, and even helps Jasmine to escape from the palace. Although he is really a gentle creature, Rajah is also great at scaring away princes who come to Agrabah hoping to marry Jasmine.

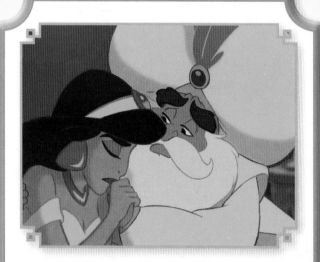

Sultan

The Sultan is a kind man and he is desperate for Jasmine to marry a prince so that she has someone to look after her. Like his daughter, the Sultan enjoys adventure and he takes a thrilling ride on Aladdin's magic carpet.

Jasmine's black hair is so long that she can sit on it! It takes her an hour every night just to brush it.

Feisty Jasmine is not frightened of Jafar. Although the wicked vizier has the Sultan where he wants him, the princess tells him that he will need to look for a new job when she rules Agrabah!

Kindred Spirits

From the moment they meet, there is a spark between Jasmine and Aladdin. They share a love of adventure and both feel trapped. Jasmine does not care whether Aladdin is a prince—he is just the most interesting person she has ever met.

Independent Lady

The law says that Jasmine must marry a prince—and soon— but Jasmine would prefer to marry for love. She is not the kind of girl who does things just because people tell her she must. Jasmine thinks the law is wrong, so she decides to change it.

Harem pants are high fashion in Agrabah. The light, silky material keeps Jasmine cool in the desert heat.

CLEVER GIRL
Jasmine has some hidden talents. She can vault across a rooftop as nimbly as Aladdin.

- ♥ *Home:* High on a rooftop in Agrabah
- ♥ *Likes:* Helping others
- ♥ *Dislikes:* Being poor and hungry

Aladdin

Life is tough for Aladdin on the streets of Agrabah. His clothes are shabby, he has to steal just to get enough food to eat, and he always seems to be running away from someone. Aladdin dreams of being rich—he thinks it would solve all his problems.

Aladdin is always willing to share with people in need. The kind street rat can't bear to see these poor children go hungry, so he gives them the bread he has just "acquired" in the market.

Diamond in the Rough

Most people don't know the real Aladdin. The street urchin only steals because he has to—really he is a kindhearted young man with a passion for adventure and fun. When he finds the magic lamp, Aladdin has a chance to show the world what kind of man he is. It just takes him a while to work it out for himself!

Prince Ali

Aladdin uses his first wish to transform himself into a prince so that he can win Jasmine's heart. He doesn't know that he already has!

Aladdin is determined to make himself worthy of a princess. However, he learns that just being himself is all that Jasmine needs.

"I gotta be smooth, cool, confident."

Abu

Aladdin's best pal is his pet monkey, Abu. The street-smart pair understand each other and Abu always looks out for his friend. However, Abu isn't very impressed when the Genie transforms him into an elephant!

The Mysterious Marketplace

FRESHEST FRUIT IN AGRABAH

TANTALIZE YOUR TASTE BUDS WITH THE JUICIEST FRUIT THIS SIDE OF THE RIVER JORDAN.

PIPING HOT!

This may look like just a regular pipe, but it can brew you a strong cup of coffee and even chop potatoes into fries. That's breakfast and dinner sorted!

Roll up, roll up! Whether you are in need of some fresh fruit, jewels for your tiara, or simply want to be entertained, the mysterious marketplace in Agrabah has everything you need. Come on in and prepare to be dazzled!

Colorful carpets.

Handwoven baskets, perfect for carrying your fruit home in.

AGRABAH'S NO.1 SNAKE CHARMER

PREPARE TO BE CHARMED!

WATCH IN AMAZEMENT AS THE MAGICAL PIPE CHARMS THE SNAKE OUT OF HIS BASKET.

FOR ONE NIGHT ONLY

YOU WON'T BELIEVE YOUR EYES!

HE'S HARD AS NAILS! HE FEELS NO PAIN! HE'S MR. BED OF NAILS!

- ♥ *Home:* Inside an old magic lamp
- ♥ *Likes:* Making people's dreams come true
- ♥ *Dislikes:* Living in a small space

The Genie

Living inside a tiny magic lamp means that the Genie doesn't get out much. In fact, unless someone rubs his lamp, the Genie doesn't get out at all! So, when Aladdin discovers the lamp, the Genie is determined to make the most of his opportunity.

Powerful One

The Genie is one-of-a-kind. He can do virtually anything (except make people fall in love, kill someone, or bring back the dead). The Genie also has a powerful personality and loves to showcase his talents through song and dance routines.

The Genie's dearest wish is to be set free so that he can travel the world. Living inside a tiny lamp cramps his body and his style.

The Genie's heart is almost as big as his personality. He is prepared to sacrifice his own freedom so that Aladdin can use his final wish to remain a prince. Thankfully, Aladdin doesn't listen to him.

New Master

One of the worst things about being a genie is that you can't choose your master. When Jafar rubs the lamp, the Genie has to follow his orders.

"Your wish is my command."

Sidekick

There are lots of magical things in the Cave of Wonders. The Magic Carpet seems to be an old chess buddy of the Genie's, and the magical pair make an entertaining team.

In-Genie-us

The Genie loves to spice things up with a little play-acting. Here are some of his most outrageous guises.

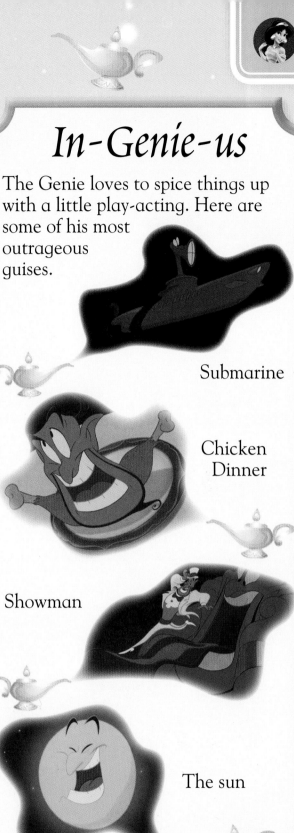

Submarine

Chicken Dinner

Showman

The sun

Waiter

Jafar

- ♥ *Home:* In the Sultan's palace in Agrabah
- ♥ *Likes:* Being in charge, getting his own way
- ♥ *Dislikes:* Having to pretend to serve the Sultan

The Sultan is happy to leave most of the running of his country to his trusted vizier, Jafar. However, Jafar has a secret agenda—he thinks he would make a much better Sultan. And when he finds the magic lamp, there will be no stopping him!

"I wish to rule on high, as Sultan."

Secret Power

Jafar uses his magical serpent staff to hypnotize the Sultan. One look into the serpent's eyes and the Sultan will agree to anything.

Sly Iago, Jafar's parrot, comes up with a brilliant plan to make Jafar even more powerful—he should marry Jasmine! Jafar loves the idea, but Jasmine does not.

Selfish Vizier

Jafar's greatest wish is to be all-powerful. He will do whatever it takes to find the magic lamp and doesn't care about anything or anyone else.

Iago

Jafar's parrot pretends to be dumb most of the time, but secretly he is a chatterbox and as evil as his master. Iago particularly hates the Sultan—well, he keeps on stuffing crackers into Iago's beak!

Evil Mastermind

When Jafar becomes Sultan, he believes that he has beaten Aladdin. But he has underestimated the street rat. Aladdin is able to trick Jafar into making a wish to become the most powerful being in the world—a genie. Jafar gets the power he always wanted, but is trapped inside a tiny lamp forever.

The Bayou

Faraway Lands

The princesses have seen some amazing sights on their travels. They can't wait to tell their friends and family all about their exciting news. So pack a bag and join the princesses on their wonderful adventures.

Dear Rajah,

The Cave of Wonders really is full of the most wondrous sights! Sparkly jewels and golden treasures. But best of all, a Magic Carpet!

Princess Jasmine

P.S. The entrance is shaped like a tiger's head!

Rajah the Tiger,
The Royal Palace,
Agrabah

Hi-ho from the little cottage!

Greetings!

Dear Charlotte,

The Bayou is beautiful (if a little smelly)! I have made lots of friends and found out that alligators aren't scary at all. When it gets dark, the friendly firefly bugs light up and guide us down the river. See you soon,

Tiana

Charlotte LaBouff,
The LaBouff Mansion,
New Orleans,
Louisiana

Dear Flounder,

I'm having a whale of a time here on dry land! I've found I love to dance and there are beautiful places to walk to. There are no scary sharks here! I have found lots of new objects to add to my collection, including a pretty clip for my hair.

Ariel

Flounder the Fish,
Under a rock,
Atlantica,
The Ocean

Wish you were here...

POCAHONTAS' STORY

ONCE UPON A TIME...

...in the year 1607, a ship set sail for the "New World" of America. With Captain John Smith at the helm, the sailors were sure they would find adventure! As for any "savages" they came across, they would teach the friendly ones to live like the British—and fight off the rest with their guns. But as Governor John Ratcliffe told his assistant, Wiggins, he only cared about finding gold for himself and his dog, Percy.

The Powhatan tribe in America were wary and wanted to protect their land for future generations. But for Pocahontas, daughter of Chief Powhatan, the future was a mystery. Should she marry Kocoum, as her father wished, or follow her own dreams? Her best friend, Nakoma, thought Kocoum was handsome. But Pocahontas was sure her dreams were trying to tell her something. In her dream, an arrow spun round and round, then stopped. "This spinning arrow is pointing you down your path," Grandmother Willow told her. But Pocahontas didn't know what it was pointing to.

When the sailors landed on Virginia, Captain Smith went to see what dangers lurked in the forest. What he found was Meeko the raccoon, Flit the hummingbird, and Pocahontas! Beautiful and intelligent, she was nothing like the "savages" he expected to find.

As they got to know each other, Smith and Pocahontas began to fall in love. They both realized that the Powhatan tribe and the Englishmen could live in peace if they would just listen to each other. Chief Powhatan promised he would listen if Captain Smith wanted to talk. But before Smith reached the village, fighting broke out—and a sailor, Thomas, shot and killed Kocoum. John Smith was captured, to be executed the following dawn. Both sides prepared for battle.

As dawn approached, Pocahontas began to realize her true path: The arrow in her dream was pointing to John Smith! She hurried to him, throwing herself over his body moments before Powhatan's club was to fall. At last, Powhatan agreed to choose a path of peace instead of war, and released Captain Smith.

But Governor Ratcliffe was not convinced. He aimed a gun at Powhatan and fired. As Smith leaped to protect the chief, he was badly wounded by the bullet. He and Pocahontas were finally together—but they had to make a difficult decision: John Smith chose to return home to get well, and Pocahontas chose to stay with her tribe, where she was needed.

As the ship prepared to leave, the Powhatans assured Captain Smith that he would always be welcome. Pocahontas waved goodbye while the ship sailed away, with a promise that she and John Smith would always be together in their hearts.

- **LIKES:** Exploring, nature, swimming
- **DISLIKES:** People destroying nature
- **FRIENDS:** Nakoma, Grandmother Willow, Meeko, Flit

POCAHONTAS

Like the rest of the Powhatan tribe, Pocahontas feels at home in nature—with the rugged mountains, moonlit woods, and flowing waters. But despite the advice of her father and friends, Pocahontas isn't interested in being like the steady river. Instead of taking the safe, stable path, she wants to run wild and free!

Pocahontas is a free spirit and loves to discover unexplored places. It is exciting to see what new adventures wait around the next bend!

HER OWN PATH

Everyone, including her father Chief Powhatan, seems to have Pocahontas' future mapped out for her. But Pocahontas is determined to follow her own heart and her own destiny.

DIFFERENT WORLDS

Proud Pocahontas won't let anyone insult her culture. She shows John Smith that although he might know all about "civilization," she has plenty to teach him about life!

"I THINK MY DREAM IS POINTING ME DOWN ANOTHER PATH."

Her mother hoped Pocahontas would wear this necklace on her wedding day.

Not just anyone can keep up with adventurous Pocahontas! Tiny Flit flies close to her side, doing his best to keep his best friend out of danger.

NEW DIRECTIONS
Pocahontas dreams of a spinning arrow. Its meaning is a mystery... until she meets John Smith!

NATURE'S STUDENT

Pocahontas is strong and wise, just like her mother before her. But she wants to take a different path to the one her mother chose. Pocahontas listens to nature's spirits with her ears and her heart. She knows that nature's lessons can teach her all she needs to know.

Pocahontas' dress is short and comfortable. She can swim in it, too!

PROTECTING LOVE
Fearless Pocahontas risks her own life to save John Smith and end the anger and hatred between his people and hers.

POWHATAN TRIBE

The Powhatan tribe is like a family to Pocahontas: They may not always agree, but they love and protect each other, no matter what. Pocahontas can always trust her friends to have her safety and happiness at heart.

- **HOME:** Virginia, America, river villages
- **LEADERS:** Chief Powhatan, tribal council
- **TRADITIONS:** Growing and gathering corn, interpreting dreams, respecting the earth

CHIEF POWHATAN

The great Powhatan is leader of his tribe, and Pocahontas' father. He loves his daughter, wild spirit and all. But he hopes that she will choose to settle down soon!

WISE CHIEF

Powhatan leads his people with a firm hand to keep them safe. In return, they respect his wisdom and obey his commands.

PROTECTIVE FATHER

Powhatan thinks he knows what is best for his daughter's future: A strong husband, a good home, and a quiet life with the tribe. It takes time for him to trust that she is responsible enough to choose her own way.

KOCOUM

Brave Kocoum is a hero in his tribe. He is strong as a bear and handsome, too. In fact, the only thing this talented warrior doesn't do well is smile!

When danger is near, Kocoum is always the first to volunteer to defend his village. He leads his fellow warriors with courage and has great skill with a bow and arrow.

NAKOMA

Cautious Nakoma wouldn't dream of breaking the rules—but hard as she tries, she can't convince her friend Pocahontas to follow them! Even though they sometimes disagree, Nakoma is a true friend and is always there when Pocahontas needs her.

"I DON'T WANT YOU TO GET HURT."

When Pocahontas needs to see John Smith, loyal Nakoma finds a way. She then keeps a careful watch to make sure her friend is safe.

GRANDMOTHER WILLOW'S WISDOM

LET THE SPIRITS OF THE EARTH GUIDE YOU!

SOMETIMES THE RIGHT PATH IS NOT THE EASIEST ONE.

IT SEEMS TO ME THIS SPINNING ARROW IS POINTING YOU DOWN YOUR PATH.

ALL AROUND YOU ARE SPIRITS, CHILD. THEY LIVE IN THE EARTH, THE WATER, THE SKY.

RIPPLES IN THE RIVER BEGIN SMALL, THEN THEY GROW. BUT SOMEONE HAS TO START THEM.

YOU KNOW YOUR PATH, CHILD. NOW FOLLOW IT!

POCAHONTAS TRUSTS GRANDMOTHER WILLOW TO OFFER WORDS OF WISDOM WHEN LIFE IS CONFUSING. THIS OLD WILLOW TREE HAS HAD MANY YEARS TO LEARN ABOUT THE WORLD, AND SHE IS ALWAYS HAPPY TO SHARE ADVICE.

GOVERNOR RATCLIFFE

- HOME: London and Jamestown, Virginia
- LIKES: Anything made of gold, his dog
- DISLIKES: Hard work, failure, "savages"

Governor John Ratcliffe knows that he is not well-liked—the nobles in the English court think he is a failure, and the sailors soon find out that he is greedy and mean. Even though Ratcliffe's quests for gold and glory never seem to work out, he won't give up! He is convinced that a trip to the New World will change his fortunes.

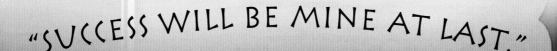

"SUCCESS WILL BE MINE AT LAST."

The sailors take control when Governor Ratcliffe reveals his true nature. Angry, scheming, and full of hatred, he refuses to listen to different opinions or change his mind.

RATCLIFFE ON PARADE

Boastful Ratcliffe makes a big show of every move he makes. When he boards the boat to the New World, he wants to be sure that everyone takes notice: Power, riches, and mountains of gold are within his reach!

WIGGINS

Wiggins is the perfect assistant to Governor Ratcliffe. He is patient, cheerful, and never seems to notice his boss' bad qualities! Hardworking Wiggins puts his best effort into every job—from scrubbing Percy the dog and praising Ratcliffe's speeches, to snipping trees into amazing animal shapes!

PERCY

Ratcliffe's beloved dog, Percy, may be the world's most pampered pooch! He enjoys long bubble baths, is carried around on a velvet cushion, and gets all the doggie treats he could ever wish for.

FLIT THE HUMMINGBIRD

Protective Flit is a friend to Pocahontas—and an enemy to anyone who might do her harm! Playful Flit might be small and quiet, but this stubborn hummingbird knows exactly how to use his long beak to get his point across.

Flit uses his super-fast flying to make speedy getaways and play mischievous pranks—like snatching a berry from Meeko!

MEEKO THE RACCOON

Meeko's favorite things are playing games, teasing Flit, and exploring with Pocahontas. His least favorite thing? Anyone who gets in the way of his snacks! He and Percy don't get along at first, fighting almost from the moment they meet. But in the end, they follow the humans' example and make peace with each other.

EXPLORER

Curious raccoons love finding shiny treasures, and Meeko boldly leaps and climbs to get them. He can't resist taking John Smith's sparkly compass!

JOHN SMITH

Bold and strong, Captain John Smith has been on countless adventures and seen lots of "new worlds." His fellow sailors admire and look up to him. They think he can succeed at just about anything. Only love can change his mind about the world he thinks he knows so well.

- **HOME:** London, and at sea
- **LIKES:** Danger, adventure, traveling
- **DISLIKES:** Staying in one place for too long

HERO

The sea captain's heroic deeds are known by all the crew on Ratcliffe's ship. Smith is sure he can tame any "savages" they find.

When young sailor Thomas falls overboard, heroic Captain Smith bravely plunges into the ocean's stormy waves to save him from drowning.

THE COMPASS

John Smith uses a compass to find his way. Its spinning arrow helps point him in the right direction—just like the arrow in Pocahontas' dream.

THOMAS

Thomas is a good man—but he wasn't much of a sailor or soldier when his ship left England. However, thanks to John Smith, he learns to be a good soldier and a leader, too.

John Smith's blond hair and blue eyes are foreign to the Powhatan people.

Thomas and Ratcliffe don't always see eye to eye. When Thomas learns to stand up for himself, he shows he is the better man.

LISTEN WITH THE HEART

To understand each other, John Smith and Pocahontas must open their hearts to new ways of seeing things. Once they do find peace and common ground, they want to show others the power of talking instead of fighting.

BACK HOME

Captain Smith is wounded while protecting Chief Powhatan, and must return to England. It is with a heavy heart that he leaves behind his beloved Pocahontas.

Unlike barefooted Pocahontas, John Smith wears heavy boots for adventuring!

Mulan's Story
Once Upon a Time...

...Chinese families prayed to their ancestors for honor and good fortune. Sons and daughters were expected to bring honor to their families, too—sons as brave soldiers; daughters as dutiful wives.

*F*a Mulan wanted to please her mother Fa Li, her father Fa Zhou, and her Grandmother Fa, but she didn't seem to have what it took to make a graceful bride.

*T*hen the Emperor's advisor, Chi Fu, arrived with bad news: The Hun army had crossed the Great Wall and invaded China. One man was called to fight from every household. Fa Zhou had been a hero in his youth, but now he could barely walk, let alone fight. However, for the honor of his family, Fa Zhou prepared for battle. Mulan was sure her father would be killed if he joined the army, but Fa Zhou would not disobey the Emperor's command. Mulan resolved to spare her father by going to war in his place—she would disguise herself as a man and join the army.

To watch over Mulan, her ancestors called on a great stone dragon. But instead of a powerful protector, the mischievous dragon Mushu appeared and set out to accompany Mulan, together with Grandmother Fa's "lucky" cricket Cri-Kee.

At the Wu Shu camp, Mulan, now called "Ping," and the other recruits trained under Captain Li Shang, son of the famous General Li. When the time came for battle, Ping's bravery stood out. He was hailed a hero for defeating the Hun leader Shan-Yu—until an injury revealed Mulan beneath the disguise.

Mulan was cast out of the army. But then she learned that Shan-Yu and his evil falcon, Hayabusa, had survived the battle and were going to attack Imperial City, where the Emperor and Li Shang's soldiers were gathered. She had to warn her friends; but would they listen?

Mulan rushed to the city with Li Shang, and army recruits Yao, Ling, and Chien-Po, and saved the Emperor, defeating Shan-Yu once and for all! As a token of gratitude and a symbol of the great honor she brought to her family, the Emperor gave Mulan Shan-Yu's sword, a medallion, and a seat on the Emperor's council. But instead of serving on the council, Mulan chose to return home to her family.

Fa Zhou welcomed Mulan home, assuring her that being her father was all the honor he could ever want. Mulan celebrated with her father, mother, grandmother, and a surprise guest: Li Shang! After their adventure together, he had become someone dear to Mulan's heart.

Likes: Spending time with her family, new challenges

Dislikes: Girls being treated differently to boys

Favorite color: Jade

Mulan

As the only daughter of a traditional Chinese family, Mulan is expected to bring honor to her family through a good marriage. She longs to please her mother and father. But Mulan just can't seem to master the sweet manners and grace of a "proper" bride!

Mulan's dress and jewelry are a glittering example of traditional Chinese style, full of layers, color, and beautiful details.

Fa Zhou

Mulan's father would risk his life to do what is right. He hopes that Mulan will do her part to bring honor to the family. Fa Zhou believes that she will blossom into someone truly special.

In Bloom

Mulan might not be the most graceful girl, but she has a steely determination that helps her overcome any obstacle. In addition to outer beauty, Mulan has an inner glow that comes from confidence, honor, and the truth of her own strength.

Remembering details isn't easy for forgetful Mulan. Scribbled hints on her arm keep important ideas close at hand!

A Brave Choice

When her father is in danger, Mulan knows what she has to do: She is determined to join the army in disguise as Ping to save her family.

FAN FAVORITE

Mulan's paper fan is a symbol of her girlhood—but she also uses it to help defeat the evil Hun, Shan-Yu.

"It's going to take a miracle to get into the army."

Mulan trains hard and learns to fight while disguised as the boy Ping. She knows that girls are every bit as brave as boys. But will her fellow soldiers ever believe it?

A long train makes Mulan's dress more fit for a princess than a soldier. Can she honor both sides of her personality?

New Friend

Captain Li Shang has trouble accepting Mulan as both a warrior and a woman. However, there is one thing he can't deny: Mulan is one brave soldier!

101

🪭 *Home:* China

🪭 *Traditions:* Praying to the ancestors, finding love with a matchmaker

🪭 *Values:* Loyalty, courage, family, honor

"The greatest gift and honor is having you for a daughter."

Mulan's Friends and Family

Lucky Mulan has family and friends who always want the best for her. They have faith that she will find her place in life and bring them honor as she grows older. Even when Mulan chooses an unusual path, her loyal family still shows her love and kindness.

Fa Li

Mulan's gentle and ladylike mother, Fa Li, sometimes doesn't know what to do with her daughter! But she loves Mulan fiercely, and worries for her safety and happiness.

Traditions

Grandmother Fa trusts in following old rituals—but not in following rules! She gives Mulan an apple for serenity, a pendant for balance, and a cricket for luck. She also says a prayer to the ancestors for extra help.

The dinner table is a welcome retreat for the Fa family: A place to eat soup, sip tea, and enjoy some quiet time together as a family.

Fire Breather

Mushu the dragon likes to show off his "fearsome" fire breath. But the Fa ancestors aren't impressed! In fact, they demoted Mushu to the lowly job of waking the other ancestors after he failed to protect a family member.

Mushu

He might be small, but Mushu is a master planner and he has big plans for Mulan! The tiny dragon quickly becomes her trusted advisor.

As the smallest member of Mulan's group, Cri-Kee the cricket sometimes struggles to keep up. He is lucky to have good friends to help him get back to safety time and again.

Cri-Kee

Grandmother Fa thinks Cri-Kee brings good luck, but this clumsy cricket admits he can be one unlucky bug! Still, he tries to make sure all his friends have good fortune.

The Emperor

The Emperor rules over his people with great courage and pride. He bravely sends soldiers away from his palace to protect his people. But even the wise Emperor has something to learn from Mulan: The power of a girl with courage, skill, and heart.

🪭 *Home:* The Great Palace, Imperial City
🪭 *Job:* Ruler of Imperial China
🪭 *Secret weapons:* Courage, pride, wisdom

"No matter how the wind howls, the mountain cannot bow to it."

A gift from the Emperor brings huge honor to any family. Thanks to her bravery, Mulan receives two: Shan-Yu's sword and the Emperor's pendant.

His Majesty

The Emperor relies on information from his scouts and advice from his council to do a good job. But he also needs the wisdom and courage in his own heart to lead his people and see the truth—even when it is unexpected.

Chi Fu

Chi Fu earned his important job as the Emperor's advisor without any help. Jealous Chi Fu wants to make sure no one unworthy follows in his footsteps.

Shan-Yu

Never one to turn down a challenge, Shan-Yu is a man built for war and destruction. He seems as big as a mountain and has terrifying weapons to defeat his enemies. Shan-Yu leads his soldiers with an iron fist. Even his glowing yellow eyes are scary!

Home: Hun empire, north of the Great Wall

Job: Fearsome Leader of the Hun army

Secret weapons: Falcon, curved sword

Hun Warrior

This fearsome Hun warrior will do anything to prove that he is better than the Emperor. Nothing stands in his way, not even the Great Wall of China! With brute strength and keen instincts on his side, Shan-Yu is sure that he can lead his army to victory.

For the Chinese soldiers, coming face to face with the ruthless Shan-Yu is a shock. They know they may never escape!

Falcon Friend

Shan-Yu's falcon, Hayabusa, makes a good scout—he can fly and perch almost anywhere. When he squawks the signal, his master knows that it is time to attack!

Li Shang

His excellent training record and family history are promising, but this young captain will have to prove himself in battle to show he has earned his high rank. He hopes to teach his troops the value of hard work, dedication, and teamwork.

Job: Training new recruits, leading Chinese soldiers in battle

Likes: The army, serving the emperor well, seeing his troops improve

Dislikes: Liars, lazy soldiers, weakness

Born Leader

Naturally strong and handsome, Li Shang has big dreams of becoming a military hero, just like his father. This brave soldier seems destined for greatness—as long as he doesn't let his pride get in the way!

Master Teacher

When it comes to training, Li Shang demands hard work and discipline from his troops. He has one goal: To turn the new recruits into skilled soldiers fit for the Chinese army—and fast!

As a new recruit, Li Shang was number one in his training class. His amazing skill is the result of practice, practice, and more practice!

General Li

Li Shang's father, General Li, is a high-ranking member of China's army. He directs troop movements and communicates with the emperor. He also promoted his beloved son to army captain.

Brothers in Arms

The troops aren't exactly skilled soldiers when they first begin, but Li Shang soon transforms them into skilled fighters. Ping, Yao, Ling, and Chien-Po soon learn the importance of working together as a team.

"If we die, we die with honor."

Ping's Ally

Disguised as Ping, Mulan's true identity is hidden—but the kindness and bravery inside her shine through. Shang recognizes the goodness in Ping and comes to trust his new friend deeply.

With flowing hair and a long, colorful dress, Mulan looks the perfect Chinese lady.

A man's outfit is the most important part of the disguise. With all that padding, you'll look just like one of the boys.

A quick cut with a sharpened sword changes long, girlish locks to a boy-next-door hairstyle.

Put away friendly waves and sweet greetings—a real tough guy greets his fellow soldiers with muscle.

Just because you look like a man doesn't mean you have to smell like one. Take a bath... but keep a lookout!

With the walk, the talk, and the look all tied together, the change is complete!

Take time to practice a manly walk: Shoulders back, chest high, feet apart, head up. Got all that? Now, strut!

It might take a while to get the hang of spitting on the ground...

Mushu's Guide to Being a Man

Tiny tough guy Mushu knows that being a man is about attitude. You've got to walk tough, talk tough, and look tough. No one said it would be easy!

Dear Princess...

Being a princess requires many noble qualities, such as kindness, heart, and elegance. But most of all a princess needs to have a wise head beneath her tiara.

Many people look up to her and may need her help with life's little problems...

Dear Snow White,

Can you help me to stay awake? Grumpy says that I sleep too much, and even Sneezy can't wake me. I feel so sleepy all the time and my bed is so very comfortable.

Sweet dreams,
Sleepy

Everyone should get plenty of sleep, but if you need to stay awake you should take long walks in the fresh air. You could also try a VERY loud alarm clock!

Love from Snow White

Dear Belle,

My friends and I are all in love with the same wonderful guy. His name is Gaston and he's the best! He's the strongest, handsomest, bravest man in town. How can I get him to notice me?

Babette (the future Madame Gaston)

The most important thing is to get to know the real Gaston, to see if he is the right guy for you. He may be handsome, but is he kind? Sometimes real beauty can be found within.

With love, Belle

Dear Cinderella,

Now, what was I going to say? Oh yes, I remember! Can you help me become less forgetful? I am always losing things, especially my wand and it is really very annoying!

Love from the Fairy Godmother

Everyone forgets things now and then! Why don't you try attaching some ribbon to the end of your wand and fixing it to your sleeve? You'll never lose it and may even start a new fashion!

Lots of love, Cinderella

Dear Tiana,

People keep on judging me by the way I look. I want to know how a big ol' gator like me can play in a swinging jazz band without scaring folk away!

Hope you can help,
Louis

A talent like yours should not be wasted. You can play at my restaurant any time and people will learn to love the real you, just like I do.

Love from Tiana

Tiana's Story

Once Upon a Time...

...in New Orleans, there lived two little girls. Charlotte, who lived with her father, Big Daddy LaBouff, wished to become a princess. Tiana hoped to open her own restaurant. Her father encouraged her and taught her to cook. He also taught her about how good food brings people together for good times. When she grew up, Tiana still had the dream of owning a restaurant, though her father had passed away. She worked extra-hard for enough money to buy the old sugar mill that they had chosen as the spot for the restaurant. But the deal fell through when someone else offered a higher price.

Across town, Prince Naveen of Maldonia and his valet, Lawrence, arrived. Charlotte made plans to marry the prince, but Dr. Facilier, the magic man, had his own plans for Naveen and Lawrence. He offered to use magic to help Naveen become rich again, but it was a trick to get rich himself. Naveen was changed into a frog and Lawrence was disguised as the prince.

At the ball held in the prince's honor, the frog prince met Tiana, who was dressed as a princess. He hoped a kiss from her would turn him human again—but she turned into a frog!

The two frogs were chased into the swamp where Mama Odie, with her snake Juju, told them that because Big Daddy was king of Mardi Gras, Charlotte was a princess until midnight. Mama Odie said that only the kiss of a princess would break the spell, so if Charlotte kissed Naveen, the frogs would become human again. Naveen would marry Charlotte and give Tiana the money for her restaurant. But Mama Odie warned them: Even though they thought they knew what they wanted, they had to look inside to find out what they needed. With their new friends, Louis the alligator and Ray the firefly, Naveen and Tiana returned to the city and realized they were falling in love.

Meanwhile Lawrence, as the prince, proposed to Charlotte and she accepted. But before the wedding was over, Lawrence's true identity was revealed and he was sent to jail! Meanwhile, Dr. Facilier was killed by the angry shadow spirits that he used for magic.

The real Naveen asked Charlotte to marry him. He knew he would lose Tiana, but he would be able to give her the restaurant she wanted. But Charlotte realized that Tiana and Naveen had true love and promised to kiss Naveen to make him human. However, it was too late and Naveen and Tiana were still frogs. Now they knew what Mama Odie had meant: Even without money and a restaurant, they had what they needed—love.

Naveen and Tiana were happy to stay as frogs if they could be together, and they married. Suddenly, magic swirled around them. When they married, Tiana became a princess and her kiss broke the spell! Human again, Naveen and Tiana opened Tiana's Palace together, with great music and delicious food, that brought people together for good times, just as Tiana's father had always said.

Tiana

Tiana never takes her eyes off her dream: Serving delicious gumbo and beignets to lots of happy customers at her very own restaurant. Tiana is willing to work as hard as it takes, even if that means missing out on fun with her friends. But deep inside her, there is a princess ready to have a little fun, too!

Dream: To open her own restaurant

Likes: Cooking, paying her own way

Dislikes: Laziness, wasting time

Daddy's Girl

Tiana's daddy, James, was her biggest inspiration. He taught her about delicious food and big dreams. But he and Tiana's mother, Eudora, knew that the best thing of all was the love of his family and friends.

"No one's ever done anything like this for me."

Dreamer

Tiana longs to open a restaurant, filled with people, music, and yummy food. She knows it will take hard work and planning, but wishing on a star can't hurt!

Hard at Work

Tiana isn't afraid of a little hard work— or a lot! She works so much that her friends Violet, Georgia, and Sammy only ever see her in a waitress uniform. But Tiana feels good doing a job well and getting a step closer to her dream.

Royal Green

The only palace Tiana longed for was the restaurant of her dreams. She never wanted to be a princess—let alone kiss a slimy frog! But royalty can come in surprising packages: A frog, a waitress, and a dear old friend on Mardi Gras day.

Tiana has worked hard to attain her dreams.

Lovely lily pads decorate Tiana's green dress, a reminder of her froggy days!

Kiss a Frog

According to the old fairy tale, the frog becomes a prince when he kisses a princess. But Tiana is no ordinary princess—and this is no ordinary fairy tale!

Prince Naveen's carefree attitude drives Tiana crazy! She thinks he does nothing but play. Tiana is determined to get him to help out instead.

SPICE IT UP!

Gumbo too bland? Try a few shakes of hot sauce to give this New Orleans speciality a little zing.

Charlotte

Cheerful Charlotte never gives up on her dreams. She would kiss a hundred frogs to be a princess! She is sure that good things will come her way, thanks to Big Daddy and the Evening Star. All she has to do is ask: "Please, please, please, please, please!"

Dream: To meet a charming prince and become a princess

Likes: Everything about princesses!

Dislikes: Having to wait for what she wants

Big Spender

With Big Daddy's money, Charlotte can have anything money can buy—from a closet full of pink dresses to a table full of beignets that a prince would love. But Charlotte knows that some things are priceless—like friendship and true love.

Charlotte's signature style is head-to-toe pink—and a great big smile.

Little Princess

Charlotte has wanted to be a princess since she was little. She loves fairy tales and dressing up in the princess dresses. Charlotte is sure that if she wishes hard enough, her dreams will come true!

Big Daddy

He is one of the richest, most powerful men in Louisiana, and king of Mardi Gras. But Big Daddy LaBouff can't say no to Charlotte. He loves spoiling her with dresses, puppies, and just about whatever else she wants!

Naveen

Prince Naveen loves his carefree life—playing music, dancing, and traveling from place to place, meeting beautiful girls! Maybe one day Naveen will learn to care for someone other than himself.

Prince Naveen has a smile as dazzling as the jewels in his crown.

Home: A polished-marble palace in Maldonia

Likes: Jazz music, dancing, traveling

Dislikes: Hard work, responsibility

Naveen loves flirting and dancing. With so many pretty girls in the world, he sees no need to settle down.

Frog Prince

Dashing Prince Naveen charms everyone with his bright smile and his carefree attitude. He is handsome (and he knows it!) but this pampered prince will have to grow up and stop avoiding responsibilty soon!

In the Cards

When his parents refuse to give him money, Naveen is desperate to be rich again. But Dr. Facilier's "help" is where the real trouble begins!

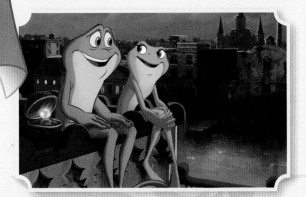

Changed Man

Froggy Tiana shows four-legged Naveen about working hard—and falling in love. He is finally ready to settle down, but he will give it all up to help Tiana get her restaurant.

How to Become a Princess

Charlotte LaBouff has wanted to be a princess since she was a little girl. She knows that wishing on the Evening Star might help—and marrying a prince! But it's also the little things that make a princess. Follow Charlotte's top tips for making all your royal dreams come true.

Top off your look with shiny jewelry for extra-special princess pizzazz and sparkle.

Live the royal life! Make your room a mini-palace with furnishings fit for a princess.

A princess has to be brave enough to meet any challenge. Would you be able to kiss a frog?

When you're royal you have to be able to make friends with all sorts of princes and princesses.

Pretty as a Picture

Charlotte knows that making a regal impression means getting every detail right. Tiara? Check. Beauty mark? Check. Perfect pink lips? Check. Matching fan? Check. Now Princess Charlotte is ready to walk the royal red carpet!

Everything you need to know about princesses is in this book! Beautiful dresses, true love, and saving princes in need.

- *Home:* The mossy swamps of Louisiana
- *Like:* Music, cruising on the river
- *Favorite foods:* Gumbo, etouffée, pralines, sauce piquant

Bayou Buddies

Deep in the bayou live critters, creatures, and bugs unlike anywhere else in the world! Bayou country is home to music-loving Cajuns, mysterious magic, and surprising friends around every turn.

Louis

He may look big and scary, but friendly Louis the alligator is a gentle giant. Like Naveen, carefree Louis doesn't let troubles get him down. He just wants to take it easy and play his horn!

Blow, Louis!

Louis has heard all the best musicians play on passing riverboats. He learned to play all the jazz classics on his trumpet, Giselle.

Louis' huge body and sharp teeth would scare anyone, but his heart is gentle!

Sticky Situation

When trouble comes his way, this scaredy-gator runs away. Ducking for cover sometimes lands Louis in trouble—and in sticky burrs!

Music-loving Ray can play a caterpillar like an accordion!

Brave little Ray knows no fear. He isn't afraid to fly to the rescue any way he can—even up a hunter's nose!

Ray

Raymond the firefly is brave, kind, and bright! With his glowing tail and a big Cajun family also ready to shed light on any situation, Ray gets Naveen and Tiana out of some tight spots. Ray is a true romantic and helps his friends learn to show their love for each other.

Love Bug

Ray sings every night to his beloved Evangeline, the brightest firefly in the sky. He doesn't know his "girl" is actually the Evening Star!

Mama Odie

Mama Odie and her pet snake, Juju, live in a shrimp boat that is wedged in a tree on the swamp. She uses her magical powers and potions to help people get not just what they want, but what they truly need.

She may be blind, but at 197 years old, Mama Odie has seen a lot of life.

Magical Gumbo

Mama Odie's gumbo doesn't just taste good—it has magical powers, too!

Dr. Facilier

Job: Telling fortunes and granting wishes in Jackson Square and his magic shop

Likes: Money, power

Dislikes: Being ignored by the rich people in town

Dr. Facilier sells magical spells to people looking for a quick fix to their problems. But his customers sometimes get more than they bargained for! Dr. Facilier works with bad magic. He will do anything to make himself rich and powerful.

Shadows

The shadows that work for Dr. Facilier are strong and sneaky. They are under his power as long as he can pay them. But if he loses control, look out!

Take a Card

Dr. Facilier has many tricks up his sleeve, including magic cards that can tell people their past, present, and future.

Shadow Man

Dr. Facilier puts on a show to convince customers to buy his spells. He will promise power, riches, and even a new head of hair. He is all smiles until he has the money safely in his hands!

"You're in my world now!"

Lawrence

Naveen's valet, Lawrence, has had enough of his boss's careless ways. Lawrence has spent years running errands, carrying bags, and racing to keep up with the prince. Now, he thinks it is his turn for a holiday!

Dr. Facilier convinces Lawrence that he can get back at his boss and take over the crown. To Lawrence, it seems like a deal too good to pass up.

Bag Man

Every time Prince Naveen breezes into a new town, his worn-out valet, Lawrence, is behind him, struggling to carry the royal wardrobe. These heavy bags have been all over the world—and Lawrence feels like he has carried them the whole way.

Prince Lawrence?

Dr. Facilier uses his magic to make Lawrence look like Prince Naveen. Now he will get a taste of the good life. Sitting at a shady table with a beautiful girl is a nice change from serving lunch!

123

Sleeping Beauty

Aurora thought she was dreaming when her prince kissed her, saving her from the sleeping curse. He risked his life to be with his love and bravely defeated the mean Maleficent. He is Aurora's hero!

Pocahontas

Pocahontas follows her own path, which leads her to a handsome stranger. They come from different worlds, but still have lots in common. She hopes they can have many adventures together in the future.

Ariel

One kiss from the handsome human and Ariel felt like she was walking on air! In return for saving his life, this keen sailor didn't think twice about saving his princess from the wicked Ursula.

Princess Tiana

Tiana works hard for what she wants. But when a charming prince comes to town, he reminds her how to have fun. Tiana realizes that what she needs most is love.

Find Your Prince

For the princesses, finding the prince of their dreams hasn't been an easy journey. After all, the path of true love never did run smooth. But the princesses listened to their hearts and with a magical kiss, found their one true loves. Follow the love hearts to find which princess matches with which prince.

Prince
Phillip

Prince
Eric

John
Smith

Prince
Naveen

Princess Jasmine
and Aladdin

Mulan and Li Shang

Pocahontas and
John Smith

Aurora and
Prince Phillip

*"He's very
handsome, isn't he?"*

Ariel and Prince Eric

Tiana and
Prince Naveen

Cinderella and
Prince Charming

Belle and the Beast

"It's more than
I ever hoped for."

Snow White
and the Prince

Happily Ever After

It has been the journey of a lifetime
for the princesses. They have listened
to their hearts, been dazzled by
magic, and dared to dream. Most
importantly, the princesses have
learned to believe in themselves.
They know that if you believe
hard enough, one day your
dreams might just come true.

Acknowledgments

LONDON, NEW YORK, MELBOURNE,
MUNICH, AND DELHI

Editors *Jo Casey, Victoria Taylor*
Designers *Thelma Robb, Anne Sharples,*
Lisa Sodeau, Nicola Erdpresser
Senior Editor *Laura Gilbert*
Senior Designer *Lynne Moulding*
Managing Editor *Catherine Saunders*
Art Director *Lisa Lanzarini*
Publishing Manager *Simon Beecroft*
Category Publisher *Alex Allan*
Production Editor *Siu Yin Chan*
Production Controller *Nick Seston*

Jacket Artist *Sara Nicolucci Storino*

First published in the United States in 2010
by DK Publishing
375 Hudson Street
New York, New York 10014

10 11 12 13 14 10 9 8 7 6 5 4 3 2 1
DD542—09/10

DK books are available at special discounts when purchased in bulk for
sales promotions, premiums, fundraising, or educational use.

For details, contact:
DK Publishing Special Markets, 375 Hudson Street, New York,
New York 10014
SpecialSales@dk.com

A catalog record for this book is available from the Library of Congress.

ISBN: 978-0-7566-6685-9

Color reproduction by MDP, UK
Printed and bound in Singapore by Star Standard

Acknowledgments
The publisher would like to thank the following people: Lauren Kressel,
Chelsea Nissenbaum, and Shiho Tilley at Disney Publishing, and Sara
Nicolucci Storino for the jacket artwork

Discover more at
www.dk.com

Snow White